Atheneum Books for Young Readers

An imprint of Simon & Schuster Children's Publishing Division

1230 Avenue of the Americas, New York, New York 10020

First published in London in 2003 by Andersen Press

First U.S. edition, 2004

Book design by Kristin Smith

The text for this book is set in Century Schoolbook.

The illustrations for this book are rendered in pen, ink, and watercolor.

Manufactured in Italy

2 4 6 8 10 9 7 5 3 1

Library of Congress Cataloging-in-Publication Data

Willis, Jeanne.

I hate school / Jeanne Willis ; illustrated by Tony Ross.—1st American ed.

p. cm.

"An Anne Schwartz Book."

Summary: Honor Brown describes all the things she hates about school.

ISBN 0-689-86523-6

[1. Schools—Fiction. 2. Humorous stories. 3. Stories in rhyme.]

I. Ross, Tony, ill. II. Title.

PZ8.3.W6799Ih 2004

[E]—dc21

2003011355

I hate School

Jeanne Willis / Tony Ross

An Anne Schwartz Book

Atheneum Books for Young Readers

New York London Toronto Sydney Singapore

There was a fine young lady,
And her name was Honor Brown.
She didn't want to go to school.
She hoped it would burn down.

And when I asked the child why,
Her little face turned red.
She threw her school hat on the floor,
And this is what she said:

"My teacher is a warty toad!
My classroom is a hole!

"The cafeteria ladies feed us worms,

And rabbit poo, and coal!"

And I believed her, every word,
For why should Honor lie,
And cling to Mother on the step,

And stamp her feet and cry?

No wonder that she made a fuss
And didn't want to go—
But surely she had lovely friends?
Young Honor Brown cried, "No!

"I've heard they cut your head off
If you're talking during class."

"They throw us out of windows,
    And they make us walk on glass.

Weren't the lessons lots of fun?
And hadn't she learned to write?

"Oh, no!" she said.
"We don't do that.
Our wrists are bound
too tight!

"My friends are crooks and villains.
They are pirates! They are bad!

"They are scary, spooky creatures.
They are monsters! They are mad!

They tied me to a rocket
And they sent me into space."

No wonder little Honor Brown
Had such a grumpy face.

"But what about the sandbox
 And the wading pool?" I sighed.
"They *would* be fun," she said,
"Except they smell like something's died.

"The sandbox is a soggy swamp.
We sit in it and sink!
The wading pool has sharks in it.
They are *killer* sharks, I think."

"You liked the field trip, surely?
You had such a happy time."

She said, "I never did, you know.
The bus was full of slime.

"A tiger ate our teacher,
    And it dragged her to its hut.

But far, far, far, far worse than that,

"The ice-cream store was shut!"

Poor Honor Brown, poor little lamb!
They made her go each day.
The first year was the worst, she said.
She didn't want to stay.

The teacher stood her on the roof
Out in the snow and rain.
And when Honor fell off, frozen stiff,
She sent her up again!

Her second year was dreadful.

On her Field Day afternoon
A wicked witch pushed past her,
And her egg fell off its spoon.

Last May a nasty monster came
And scribbled on her work,

And no one would believe her;
All the teachers went berserk.

Yes, Honor Brown just hated school.
She hated it for years.
Yet on the day that she could leave,
I found her full of tears.

"Whatever's wrong?" I asked her.
"You no longer have to go."
But Honor Brown just howled
And sobbed,

"I'll really *miss* it, though!"